Yawn and stretch, hop out of bed
as the morning sun appears.

Wake up, Mom! Wake up, Dad!
The Easter Bunny was here!

The bunny brought us presents,
he left eggs outside and in.

Put on your shoes and grab a bag—
let the Easter hunt begin!

Beneath the bushes, under leaves,
eggs are hidden around.

Search and find, collect them all,
until each one is found.

And now we look for the baskets.
What goodies did we get?

Chocolate, toys, more jelly beans...
it's the greatest Easter yet!

The hunt is done, we found it all,
and now it's time for play.

Blow some bubbles, fly a kite,
Easter is the greatest day!

It's time to come inside
to brush our teeth and comb our hair.

Mom says church won't wait—
we need to go and say our prayers.

We put on our best clothes
since it's a very special day.

Then Mom and Dad take pictures
before we're on our way.

Easter service with family—
together we pray and sing.

We leave church filled with a love
that only this day can bring.

Back at home, the ham is cooking;
the rolls are baking, too.

The family will be over soon
and there's still so much to do!

Finally it's time to eat
and Grandpa wants to pray.

"Thank you, Jesus, for giving us
this very special day."

"Today is the day we celebrate
how you died then lived again.

We thank you for your sacrifice
and forgiving all our sins."

"Jesus died and lived again.
But Grandpa, how can that be?"

"Well, sweetheart, it's like a caterpillar,
with its cocoon growing on the tree."

"It leaves its former body behind,
but it hasn't gone to die.
Instead through nature's wonder,
it becomes a butterfly!"

"And Jesus came back too,
in a different wondrous way.
He watches us from high above,
each and every day."

While we enjoy our meal and gifts
we should remember that on this day

Jesus came back like a butterfly.
He changed but hasn't gone away.

God's loving grace is everywhere,
from the ground up to the sky.

Celebrate the joys of Easter,
and look for the butterfly.

P.O. Box 4410, Naperville, Illinois 60567-4410
(630) 961-3900
Fax: (630) 961-2168
sourcebooks.com

Source of Production: Leo Paper, Heshan City, Guangdong Province, China
Date of Production: November 2017
Run Number: 5010630

Printed and bound in China.
LEO 10 9 8 7 6 5 4 3 2 1